Level 4

Re-told by: Mo Sanders
Series Editor: Rachel Wilson

Pearson Education Limited
KAO Two
KAO Park, Harlow,
Essex, CM17 9NA, England
and Associated Companies throughout the world.

ISBN: 978-1-2923-4680-9

This edition first published by Pearson Education Ltd 2020

1 3 5 7 9 10 8 6 4 2

Set in Heinemann Roman Special, 14pt/23pt
Printed by Neografia, Slovakia

Published by Pearson Education Limited

Acknowledgments
123RF.com: Kitchner Bain 22, Simon Eeman 22
Getty Images: Anup Shah 27, Cheryl Ramalho 26, ChristianNasca 24, Gallo Images-Dave Hamman 27, Pawel Kowalczyk / EyeEm 27
Shutterstock.com: Bildagentur Zoonar GmbH 24, Federica Cordero 22, Sunshine Seeds 22

For a complete list of the titles available in the Pearson English Readers series, visit www.pearsonenglishreaders.com.

Alternatively, write to your local Pearson Education office or to Pearson English Readers Marketing Department, Pearson Education, KAO Two, KAO Park, Harlow, Essex, CM17 9NA

In This Book

Simba

The young son of Mufasa

Nala

Simba's friend

Mufasa

The king of the Pride Lands

Scar

Mufasa's brother

Timon

A meerkat in the jungle

Pumbaa

A warthog and Timon's best friend

Before You Read

Introduction

Simba looks down on the Pride Lands with his father. "One day you are going to be king of all this," Mufasa tells him. But Simba's uncle, Scar, and his hyena friends have a different plan. Can Simba follow the great kings of the past? Who will be the Lion King?

. . . .

Activities

1 **Read the sentences and say True or False. You can use the Glossary on pages 22–23.**

1 Lions eat plants.

2 Hyenas eat meat.

3 Lions live in cold places.

4 Meerkats are smaller than lions.

2 **Look at page 1 of the story and answer. What are they?**

1 Grandfather and grandchild

2 Father and son

3 Two friends

Mufasa was king of the Pride Lands. He was also Simba's
father. Simba liked to sit on the high rock with his father. The
two lions looked down on all the lands below them.
"One day you're going to be the king of all this," Mufasa told
his son. Then, Mufasa told Simba about the great circle
of life.

But Mufasa's brother Scar wanted to be king. He told Simba about a place outside the Pride Lands. There were elephant bones there.

"But it's a secret. Please don't go there," said Scar. "It's very dangerous for young lions."

Simba was excited. He wanted to know more about the dangerous place. Scar smiled. Secretly, he wanted Simba to go there.

Simba told his best friend Nala about the secret place.
"We're going to the water," they told their mothers.
That was not true—they went all the way to the
secret place.
"Look at all the elephant bones!" said Nala.
The two young lions were excited and afraid. Then they heard
a terrible noise …

Suddenly, three hyenas stood in front of them. "This is *our* place," one hyena said. "We *eat* little lions who come here." The hyenas laughed. Simba and Nala were scared. They ran away fast. But the three hyenas ran after them, and they were faster.

Suddenly … *ROAR!* Mufasa was there! The hyenas turned and ran from the Lion King.

"I'm sorry, Dad," Simba told Mufasa later that night. He didn't want his father to be angry with him.

Mufasa pointed to the night sky. "Simba, look up at the stars," he said. "The great lion kings of the past look down on us from up there. Those kings are always going to be there for you."

One day, Scar took Simba into a deep valley.

"Wait here," he said. "You're going to get a surprise."

Scar left and Simba waited for the surprise. He was excited.

Suddenly, he heard a sound—feet, hundreds and hundreds of feet. Was this the surprise?

Simba looked around. There were hundreds of wildebeests running through the valley.

It was a stampede! Simba was very afraid. He tried to run, but there was no safe place in the valley. *"Help!"* he shouted. Suddenly, Mufasa was there. The King of the lions pushed his way through the wildebeests. He carried Simba in his mouth and put him on a rock high above the stampede.
Simba was safe there.

Mufasa tried to climb up a bigger rock. He looked up and saw Scar at the top.

"Help me, Brother," said Mufasa. But Scar only smiled.

"*I'm* going to be the Lion King now," he said. Then he pushed Mufasa down to the stampede below them.

From his rock, Simba couldn't see any of this.

After the stampede, Simba climbed down into the valley.
"Dad?" he called.
Then he saw Mufasa's body and understood—his
father was dead.

Scar walked slowly into the valley. "What did you do?"
he asked.
"It was an accident," answered Simba. He was afraid. "What
can I do?"
"*Run*," said Scar. "Run away and never come back."

Simba ran and ran. He was scared and sad. Simba left the Pride Lands and started to run across the desert.

After hours with only desert all around him, he couldn't run any more. He was hungry, and thirsty, and tired.

He fell to the ground and slept.

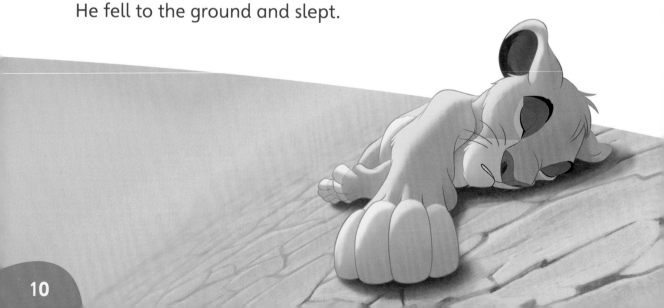

After some time, Simba opened his eyes and saw two animals standing over him—a warthog and a meerkat.

"He isn't dead!" cried Pumbaa the warthog.

"Lions eat meerkats!" said Timon the meerkat. "But perhaps this lion can be our friend. Friends don't eat friends."

It was the start of a different life for Simba, with his two new friends.

Simba lived with Timon and Pumbaa for many years. He became a big lion.

One day, the three friends were in a new part of the jungle. Suddenly, a lioness jumped out at Pumbaa.

"Help!" cried the warthog. "She's going to eat me!"

Simba heard his friend and jumped between the lioness and the warthog.

The two lions started to fight. But then Simba stopped and said, "Nala?" The lioness stopped. "Simba?" she asked. The two lions started to laugh.

"What's happening here?" asked Timon. "Do you *know* her?"

"Yes! Nala was my best friend years ago!" cried Simba.

That evening, Nala told Simba about life at home.

"Scar is king now, and the hyenas work for him," she said.

"There's no food and no water for the animals. Life is terrible. Simba, you must go back and help. You are the true king!"

"I'm *not* the king!" Simba cried. "And I *can't* go back!" He walked away angrily.

"Nala doesn't understand," Simba said. "I can *never* go back. I can't change the past."

He remembered Mufasa's words to him from years ago and looked up at the dark sky. "You said to me—'I'm always going to be there for you.' But you're not!" he shouted. Simba wanted to see his father.

But then a deep voice said, "Simba."

Simba looked up. "Father?" The clouds above him moved into a new shape. It was Mufasa!

"I live *inside* you, Simba," the old king said. "You must remember that. You are my son and the one true king. Remember ..." The light started to go.

"Don't leave!" cried Simba. But the sky was dark again.

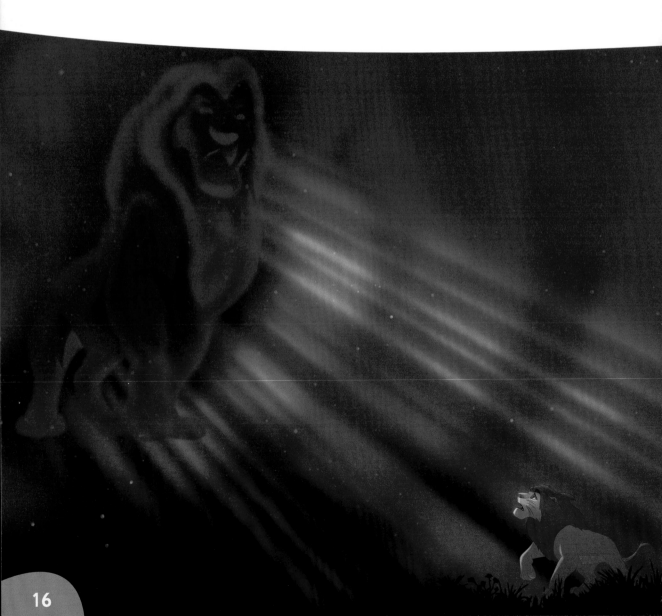

Simba understood. He couldn't run from the past. He had to go home.

Simba ran for hours across the desert. At last he came to the Pride Lands. He was surprised. Years ago it was a beautiful place. But not now …

Simba looked behind him. Nala, Timon, and Pumbaa were there. "Friends help their friends," said Timon.

Simba found Scar on the high rock. "*I'm* the king now,"
Simba told his uncle.

But Scar said, "Tell all the animals your secret. *How* did
Mufasa die?"

"It … was an accident," Simba cried.

Suddenly, Scar pushed him back off the rock. Simba nearly
fell but he held on to the top of the rock with his front paws.

"Here's *my* little secret," said Scar quietly. "I killed Mufasa!"
At the sound of these words, Simba became stronger. He
jumped up from the rock and fought Scar. Scar was strong.
But Simba was stronger and faster. He pushed Scar down.
"Say it louder!" he shouted.
"I KILLED MUFASA!" shouted Scar.
"Now run," Simba said. "Run away and never come back."

It was the start of a new time. Simba was the Lion King now, and Nala was the Queen.

They stood on the high rock with their new son and looked down at the Pride Lands. Simba remembered his father's words. There was a circle of life, and now Simba was a part of that circle.

After You Read

1 **Read the sentences and say True or False.**

1 Simba is the king at the start of the story.
2 Mufasa tells Simba about a secret place with animal bones.
3 There is a wildebeest stampede in the desert.
4 Scar kills his brother.
5 Simba is afraid of Nala.
6 Simba tells Scar to run away.

2 **Match the characters and the words.**

1 "Friends don't eat friends."   **3** "I can't change the past."
2 "You are the true king!"   **4** "I killed Mufasa!"

3 **Read and discuss with a friend. Explain your answers.**

1 Who is your favorite character in the story?
2 Who is the funniest character?
3 What is the most exciting part of the story?
4 What is the saddest part?

Glossary

bone (*noun*) the hard parts inside the body

dead (*adj.*) not living any more; *Then he saw Mufasa's body and understood—his father was dead.*

desert (*noun*) land where it is hot and dry and there is not much water or many plants

hyena (*noun*) an African animal like a dog, that eats meat

jungle (*noun*) a thick forest in a hot place with many large plants

kill past tense **killed** (*verb*) to make a person or animal die; *"I KILLED MUFASA!" shouted Scar.*

lioness (*noun*) a female lion

hyena

meerkat

warthog

wildebeest

meerkat (*noun*) a small African animal that eats meat and plants

paw (*noun*) an animal's foot

safe (*adj.*) not in danger; *He tried to run, but there was no safe place in the valley.*

secret (*noun*) a thing that only a small number of people know and do not tell others about

stampede (*noun*) a large number of animals running fast

valley (*noun*) the lower land between the mountains

voice (*noun*) the part of the body you use to speak

warthog (*noun*) an African animal that eats plants

wildebeest (*noun*) a large African animal like a cow, that eats plants

Phonics

Say the sounds. Read the words.

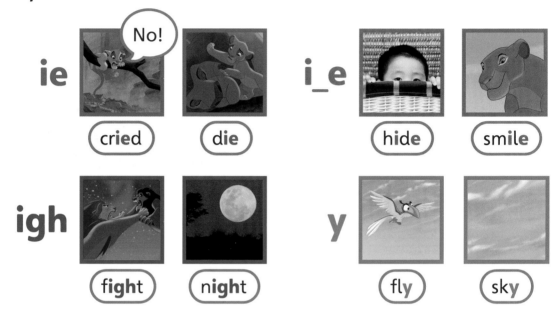

ie — cried · die

i_e — hide · smile

igh — fight · night

y — fly · sky

Say the rhyme.

Simba looked up at the stars and cried, "Why?"
Mufasa smiled down at his son from the sky.

The sun's light arrived at the end of the night,
And the true Lion King was ready to fight.

Values

Tell the truth.

All right. But you must stay in the Pride Lands.

Can Nala and I go play?

But the friends had a secret plan. They went to a new place.

What have we got here?!

Mufasa had to save the cubs.

Help!

You lied to us, Simba!

I'm sorry, Father.

Find Out

How do lions live in Africa?

Lions in Africa live on wide, open lands with a lot of grass. They live in groups of about three different families. Lions sleep for about 20 hours every day!

Lions are bigger than lionesses. They protect the group from dangerous animals.

Lionesses usually hunt for the group's meat because they are faster. They often hunt at night. Sometimes they hunt in a group and catch large animals.

a lion protecting the group

a lioness hunting a wildebeest

A mother lioness has between two and six cubs at a time.
The cubs can eat some meat at six weeks old.
Lion cubs first learn to hunt and fight by playing with their
brothers and sisters.

lion cubs with their mother